THE
ADVENTURES OF
LINDY
MANDERSON

THE ADVENTURES OF LINDY MANDERSON

Destinee Munoz

Bubba Bear Publishing

This book is a work of fiction. The names, characters and events in this book are the products of the author's imagination or are used fictitiously. Any similarity to real persons living or dead is coincidental and not intended by the author.

The Adventures of Lindy Manderson

Bubba Bear Publishing

Library of Congress Control Number: 2020950059

ISBN (paperback): 9781662907166
eISBN: 9781662907173

CONTENTS

THE ADVENTURES OF LINDY MANDERSON

Once upon a time...there was a land far, far away in the unknown state of Mickawa, Rosia. This place was called Wayn-Doddle Land. It was a place where anything can happen at any time, through the use of imagination!

In the big forest, there was a family that lived in a small, but beautiful and comfy house. The mother and the three children who lived in that house loved their state with much loyalty.

The eldest child is named Lindy Manderson. She is 12 years old. She is smart and adventurous. Not to mention, she also helps keep her siblings out of trouble.

The middle sibling is a boy named Thomas. He is 9 years old and also loves going on adventures, but he is very shy. Thomas gets nervous sometimes when he meets new people.

The youngest sibling is a boy named Ben. Ben is 8 years old and very confident. Ben is also a creator, and he likes to come up with new inventions!

Mariana Manderson is the name of the mother. She is 41 years old. She is a single mother who is kind, understanding, and strong in every situation.

This family is about to face their biggest challenge yet, and this all starts with a stranger from the past...

CHAPTER 1
THE JOURNEY BEGINS...

THE JOURNEY BEGINS...

One day, Lindy and her brothers decided to go into the forest to find some berries for their mother. You see, dear reader, Mariana caught the flu just a week ago and the kids have been taking care of her while she has been sick! Luckily, they heard rumors about a cure called "healing berries." Healing berries are bright purple berries that can heal any kind of sickness or injury.

So, they thought that if the berries were able to cure anything, it surely would cure the flu as well! On their way there, they found more and more berries on every corner. Lindy sighed.

"Okay," said Lindy as she started to walk down the path towards their house. "Now that we have the berries, Mom will feel better for sure!" As they passed the forest, Lindy and her brothers suddenly had the feeling that they were being followed or watched by someone or something.

Finally, after five long minutes, they quickly turned around. They were then met with a figure they've never seen before. It was a man. He was tall, and as skinny as a stick in a tree. He wore a brownish colored jacket that had multiple pockets from top to bottom. His hair was a mixture of both black and gold, which made him look young and old at the same time.

He had a kind expression on his face and Lindy was the kind of person who liked to trust and befriend people. So, she thought this was going to be the start of a new friendship or...at least she hoped it was.

CHAPTER 2
THE NEW ALLY AND THE NEW DISCOVERY

THE NEW ALLY AND THE NEW DISCOVERY

"Excuse me?" said the tall man as he stepped forward towards the children, "Are you kiddos lost?"

Puzzled, yet sure of where they are, Ben answered, "No, we are not lost. We were actually heading back home."

The man sighed. He wore a sad expression, although he still looked very kind.

"Oh…I just wanted to ask if you all had seen a female friend of mine. I tried asking others but they either don't know who she is or they just don't care. But I understand if you all need to get home. It's probably weird of me to ask you kids where someone is..."

As they stared at the poor man, they thought over what he had said. Immediately Lindy said, "Well, maybe if you give us her name, we can somehow help you find her." As she offered this solution, the mysterious man's face filled with joy.

He thanked them first, before telling them the name. "Her name is...Mariana Manderson and I heard rumors that she lives in these very woods."

As soon as they heard the name, the children were frozen in shock for a while. It was Thomas who finally spoke, "Wait a minute! That's our..." Thomas paused, and instead took out a picture of their mother and handed it to the man.

Once he finished looking at the picture, he looked back at the kid who gave it to him and finally said, "Y-you're...her kids and s-she's your m-mother?" Ben nodded along with Lindy and Thomas. The man smiled with joy as he BURSTS with excitement in front of the children.

Almost dropping the picture in his hands, the man started shouting happily. "OH MY GOD! T-this is incredible! I-I never thought that Mariana would actually be here a-and she even has children! I thought the rumors weren't real b-but it's really true!!"

After gushing over this information, he slowly but surely started to calm down and eventually apologized to the kids for his reaction. "Um...I guess I got a little bit excited here, sorry about that kiddos."

Lindy shook her head understandably and said, "Don't worry about it! Everyone gets surprised once in a while, mister...?"

Once he realized he didn't give his name, he immediately spoke "Oh! I forgot to introduce myself," he cleared his throat "My name is Professor Von Sticks!" He then offered his hand for a handshake.

"It is nice to meet you, Professor Von Sticks!" said Ben as he shaked his hand. He had a strong grip.

"So, do you know where she is by any chance?" asked the professor as he let go of Ben's hand.

"Well, she's at the house right now and we're bringing these berries to her," answered Lindy as she held out the berries to him.

"Hm?" said the Professor as he picked up one of the berries and examined it.

CHAPTER 3
THE
REUNION

THE REUNION

After Lindy and her brothers introduced themselves to Professor Von Sticks, they decided to take him back to their home. On the way, Lindy became curious and asked the professor, "What kind of stuff do you do as a professor?"

The professor seemed hesitant at first, but then explained it to her. "W-well, I go to different countries to search for any paranormal activities or sighting to capture them," he answered nervously.

As he explained this to Lindy, she started to feel confused so she asked him why he would want to capture ghosts.

"Um...this may sound a bit weird, but every time I would capture a ghost, I would keep them for a while just to get to know them. I would study why they do the things they do and then set them free. I believe that not every spirit is bad and they're just misunderstood!" said Professor Von Sticks with a proud expression on his face.

After a moment of silence, the professor finally asked "So, what are these berries called exactly, and what do they do?"

Lindy explained to him everything she knew about the healing berries, including the rumors she has heard because she felt the information would be useful to him. The professor seemed to be surprised but calmly said, "I bet that one day, it will change everything." Lindy was about to ask what he meant by that, but realized they had already arrived at the Manderson household.

It was a red-brick house, painted in a yellow rose color. In front of the house, there was a field of roses, daisies, dandelions, and other various flowers. In the garden, there were also a couple gnomes.

Inside the house, the walls were painted a red rose color. Infused with the red paint, were swirls of different colors. The furniture looked comfortable, and the couch pattern resembled a spring garden!

"Oooh fancy! Mari! Are you here?" yelped the professor as his excitement flowed through him.

"Shhh!" whispered Lindy as she put her finger to her lip. "We have to be quiet, Mom's sleeping right now and she gets kinda cranky when she's awake. Plus, she might not know that you're here!"

The professor felt a sense of embarrassment. "Sorry, Lindy! It's just...I haven't seen your mother in a long time and she was the only friend I had. I thought that I should catch up with her, that's all," said Professor Von Sticks as he started to reminisce about the past.

Silence filled up the entire room until Lindy finally said, "I suppose it is almost 3:00 pm and Mom should be awake by now. So, maybe you can catch up with her then." The professor smiled at the little sweet child as he sat down on the couch to wait for Mariana and Lindy. When Lindy came into Mari's room, she quietly slid in beside Mariana and whispered in a light hearted voice, "Mom, it's time to wake up." Mariana then woke up and looked at her with sleepy eyes just like a puppy.

"Already?" Mari said in a tired voice as she tried to get out of bed.

"Yeah. Oh! I need to mention, there's someone here who wants to see you," said Lindy as she helped her sleepy mother out of bed.

"Oh really? I'm not expecting anyone to visit this late, who is it?" said Mari as she started to walk to the living room. Just as she was about to enter, she froze in place once she saw the professor. Another moment of silence filled up the room until the professor slowly got up and walked towards Mariana.

"H-hello Mari, I really missed you and I'm so glad to see you again." As he was about to say more, Mariana quickly gave him a hug and started crying.

She cried tears of joy while hugging the professor, and after a while, Mariana finally let go of him and dried her tears.

CHAPTER 4
MARIANA'S STORY: PART 1

MARIANA'S STORY: PART 1

When Mariana finally calmed down, she spoke with happiness in her heart for the first time in years. "T-tommy, I can't believe it! It's really you! You're actually here!" She said as she once again hugged the professor.

"I can't believe it either, Mari. I'm happy to see you again," said the professor as he hugged her back.

"Mom, we...um got some berries that might help you," said Lindy as she handed her mom the healing berries.

"Oh, thank you, NumNums," said Mariana as she took the berries into the kitchen. She planned on making a berry soup.

Now dear reader, you're probably wondering how Mariana and Professor Von Sticks know each other. Do not worry, we will get into that right now. We're going to take a little trip to London, England where I'm going to tell you the origins of the professor and Mariana.

Mariana was 12 years old when she first met Tom, and Tom was 13 years old when he first met Mariana.

When Mariana was a little girl, she lived in a house between the forest and the village. The village was called Alma Valiente. Alma Valiente means "brave soul" in Spanish.

If you'd studied history, then you might know that in New England, the king proposed the Stamp Act, the French and Indian war, the Boston Massacre, and so much more. Yet, that didn't stop Mariana Manderson from becoming a colonist and joining The Revolutionary War. One day, Mariana was out shopping with her parents, John and Lisa Anderson.

"Hey Mari, can you get some squash and berries for me?" asked John as he held out a basket for her.

"Sure thing, Daddy," said Mariana as she grabbed the basket out of his hands. She then went to one of the market stands. As she was walking back with the squash and berries in her basket, she bumped into someone and dropped the basket onto the ground.

"Oh! Sorry, madam! Are you okay?" said a boy's voice. He held out a hand to help her up.

"Don't worry about it, I'm alright," said Mariana in a calm voice.

"That's good. Again, I'm sorry miss?" said the boy, as he wondered about her name.

"It's fine. I'm Mariana by the way; what's yours?" asked Mari.

"Nice to meet you, Mariana, I'm Tom Bucker. Want me to help you clean up the food?" asked Tom as he leaned down to grab the squashes. After picking up all the berries and squashes, they put them back in the basket. Luckily, nothing was bruised or smudged.

"Thank you, Tom," Mariana said, giving Tom a pleased smile.

"No problem, it's the least I could do for you." Tom says as he accepts her smile. "So...um if you aren't busy or anything, maybe we can hang out sometime? I know we just met, but there's not a lot of kids around here. Plus, some of the kids here...

don't really like me. You're probably the only girl who is kind to everyone." Tom explained, wearing a nervous expression.

After thinking it over for a moment, Mariana then said, "Of course, Tom! It would be nice to get to know more people my age. Like you said, there's not many kids here to play with. I also have met some kids that aren't as...kind as the adults, so this could be fun."

Before she could say any more, Mari sees her parents walking towards her as they call for her. "I have to go," she tells Tom.

Tom nodded as Mari waves at him before walking towards her parents. "Great, I'll see you later then," said Tom as he watched Mariana walk into the sunset with her parents.

CHAPTER 5
MARIANA'S STORY: PART 2

MARIANA'S STORY: PART 2

After that meeting, Mariana and Tom became best friends over the course of four months. Their parents were kind to them whenever they visited each other. Tom and Mari did everything together growing up. They would explore the woods by Mari's home, run around the meadows near the village, play with the animals in the forest, and so much more.

Mariana and John spent most of their childhood together, but now they have both grown up. Mariana is now seventeen years old and John is now eighteen years old.

One day, the doorbell rang in the Manderson household.

"I'll get it!" John said. When he opened the door, he found Tom standing outside. Tom looked like he was waiting for someone ...

"Hey Thomas! I didn't expect you to visit this afternoon. What are you here for?" asked John as he let Tom inside.

"Hello, Mr. Manderson. Is Mari here?" Tom asked as he took off his coat.

"Yeah, she's upstairs in her room drawing. You want me to go get her?" John asked, as he started climbing up the stairs.

"Sure, if that's alright with you." Tom says, as he watched John get Mariana. While Tom waits, John goes up to Mariana's room to check on her.

"Hey, Bubba-bear?" John calls. As he walks in, he sees Mari drawing a rose field.

"Hey dad! What's up?"

"I just came to tell you that Tom's here to see you," John explained.

"Thomas? That's Awesome! What's he here for?" Mari asked John as she got up.

"He didn't say, he probably wants to hang out or something," answered John as he walked downstairs with her.

Tom was excited and joyful when he saw them come down the stairs. "Hey Mari, wanna hang out today?" Tom asked as he started to get his coat.

"Heck yeah, I do! Can we, Daddy? Pleaaaase?" Mariana asked as she gave her dad the "puppy eyes."

"Alright, alright. You two can play! But if you're going to Tom's house, call me when you get there, okay?" John said, and suddenly he became a little serious.

"Okay Dad, we will." Mariana promised.

"Good, now have fun, you two!" John said.

The two said goodbye to John and began walking towards Tom's house.

CHAPTER 6
THE RUMORS

THE RUMORS

When Mariana finished cooking the berry soup, she served them to her children and Professor Von Sticks.

"Tom, where have you been all this time? I thought you were gone after the accident!" exclaimed Mari. She was shaking so hard that she almost dropped her soup.

"Well, it's kind of a long story but you don't have to worry. I'll be alright for the most part, to be honest." Tom said as he started to drink his healing berry soup.

While everyone was enjoying their soup, Mariana explained to Lindy, Ben and Thomas how she knew Tom. After explaining the situation, they tried to make sense of what just happened.

"So, let me get this straight," started Lindy as she continued to revisit this information. "You're telling me that you and Professor Von Sticks have known each other before we were born and we didn't know anything about the professor until earlier today?" Lindy asked her mother, trying to make sure she understood correctly.

"Yes, NumNums. When I was little, Tom and I suddenly bumped into each other while my parents were shopping." Mariana explained. "He was a kind boy back then, and his parents were nice to me whenever I visited them. We'd used to do everything together, and we would play in the forest where your grandparents used to live." She said with a joyful smile on her face.

"Yes, those were great memories we had, but I wanted to fill you in on what has been going on. While I was looking for you, one of the queen's knights gave me a scroll message and it is urgent!" The professor explained as he pulled out a scroll with strange writing. The professor is familiar with this writing as he studied it in college.

As the professor showed more of the message, it also revealed a mysterious map. A map of what looked to be a house somewhere outside their state.

"Uh...Tom?" Mari asked as she looked at the scroll a bunch of pictures came flying out along with bio files. "Where did you get all these pictures and files?" Tom Bucker understood why Mari was confused, so he started to explain.

"I found them before I knew you were here. I was investigating a haunted house." The professor said as he went through the biography files. "The couple that lived there had two sons and a daughter named Rose. She was 11 or 12 years old, and was a writer. Some of the files I found had pictures of the family." As he took out the photos from his bag, one of them was a drawing of a dog that looked like a husky. Hand-written below the photo was the word "Mia."

"Are you sure these are Rose's files? The pictures so far are of her family and dog, but none of herself." Mariana said, looking suspicious.

"Well, I saw some pictures of her and some of them were slightly burnt. However, that's not all I found, look at this!" He pulled a music box from his bag. It was written in English, but sounded Japanese and Spanish. "This was in one of the bedrooms and to be honest, I was confused about where it came from." The professor said with a horrified chill in his voice.

"What's so important about this box anyway?" Ben asked as he examined the box.

"You'll have to find out for yourself…" Tom said as he played the music box.

♬*A long, long time ago, the devil fell above,*
climbing up to heaven, but was soon found by me ♬

♬*He looked so alone and scared, oh how*
I showed him my mercy by giving a smile to
him, and then we walked to my home ♬

♬*My name is Rosie, I'll make sure*
you are well, there is no need to be alone
or scared, I'll take care of you here ♬

♬*And so, I took care of him, no longer lonely*
then, I knew we could be a brand new family ♬

♬*As the years passed on and on,*
we were like two crossing hearts that never
broke apart, all thanks to this miracle ♬

♬*But then came that tragic day, when*
you were taken away, it really left a mark
because my whole world went dark ♬

♬*From that moment, I took your soul*
and brought you to heaven where you would
finally be free, I thought I was free too ♬

♬*But then, the angels of heaven had*
seen me, they thought I had killed my
brother and started to fight me ♬

♫ *Instead of fighting back, I smiled and ran away back to the underground, laying in the golden flowers as I started to disappear* ♫

♫ *I'm sorry dear brother, but I will only spare them all, because I know there is good within, it just needs to be heard* ♫

♫ *I knew this 'cause I met you, we were a family and I know you're afraid to see the world, but it's not bad really* ♫

♫ *I will stay here by your side in this dark, dark place where our hearts are the only light and we will soon be free*♫ ....♡♥

When the music box stopped playing, the entire room was silent.

CHAPTER 7
THE HUNT BEGINS

THE HUNT BEGINS

Lindy finally broke the silence. "That was...really sad. Did anyone else almost cry or is it just me?" Everyone in the room responded with no while their eyes were filled with fear and confusion.

Even though Mariana and the others had no idea what just happened, Tom was quiet for some reason.

"You okay, professor?" Thomas asked as he put his hand on the professor's.

"Hm? Yeah, I'm fine. It's just that...I haven't heard this song since she showed me." Tom explained.

"Huh? What do you mean?" Mariana asked him with a puzzled look on her face. "Do you remember that girl I mentioned? That was her." The professor continued to explain. "Well, when I was looking around the abandoned house where Rose's family used to live, I thought it must've been abandoned for years. But...something strange kept happening, I have this feeling that this was somehow connected to Rose."

"But that wasn't the only thing that occurred! Whenever I would go to a certain place in the house like the basement or the office, I would hear a voice telling me not to go there. I honestly don't know why they warned me, but I'm not a risk taker like I was once was. However, the biggest encounter I've had happened when I was about to leave the house."

Everyone in the room was tense after he had stopped speaking.

"W-what happened?" Mari asked nervously.

"I don't know if I should tell you, it might be too disturbing for you all." Tom said as he felt goosebumps run down his spine. "But...I suppose I should tell you, considering you'll do anything to convince me to tell."

Tom bucker prepared himself as he continued to tell his tale. "After not finding anything, I decided to call it a night and would come back the next night. However, just when I was about to reach the doorknob, I suddenly heard another voice calling to me. It wasn't those 'keep out' voices, it was saying, 'Don't go!' I quickly turned around and I saw..." the professor stopped speaking.

Mari, Lindy, and her brothers were all eager to find out what he saw. "What did you see?" Mari and Lindy shouted as their excitement started to take over them.

"I saw a girl, but something about her felt different. Luckily, I had a flashlight with me, so I was able to see her clearly. And I swear to the Holy Lord I'm not making this up. She had curly black hair that was tied into a ponytail and she wore what looked like a dirty hospital gown." The professor explained, as he slowly started to feel the chills.

"She was somehow floating in the air! I wasn't sure where she came from, but for some reason...I wasn't scared for her. I know it sounds kinda odd and even ridiculous, but just hear me out. One thing that makes up ghosts is their aura. It is either good or bad. However, this girl's aura was both good and bad. It felt like she was trying to tell me something."

As he stopped talking for a while, Mariana, trying to stay calm, finally spoke. "Why did you go there?" she asked with absolute terror in her body.

"Well, there were rumors that at midnight, a creature known as the 'Night Demon' roams around the towns and villages. Some people claim that it only roams at night, but others have seen it during daylight, hiding in the shadows," said Tom as he pulled out the reports he had in his pocket.

"Once I heard about it, I kept having nightmares and confusing dreams about the Night Demon and the ghost girl at the abandoned house. After a while, I decided to figure out what was happening for the sake of my curiosity and also to get rid of my nightmares.

"I managed to find the information at the local library, and what I found was pretty disturbing. According to this article I found, there was a boy who ran away from home and fell here. He was found by Rose Day herself, and she took care of him for about 12 years until the boy grew ill and died from the sickness. However, the girl somehow got in the underworld and was able to bring him to heaven. After that, she suddenly disappeared."

Looking puzzled, Lindy asked him what that story had to do with the ghost girl. Professor Von Sticks then proceeds with the rest of the story. "Anyway, as I kept looking at her, I noticed how she looked similar to Rose based on the photos I found at the library. She had the same features as the ghost did." After a moment of silence, I finally asked her the question that was in my head, "'Who are you?' She managed to answer in an interesting way."

"She stopped floating and landed on the ground, signaling me to follow her. I didn't want to upset her, so I followed her upstairs to a room I haven't seen. She then pulled out a box just like this one." He then pointed at the music box on the table. "When she showed me this, I was a bit confused at first. I did not understand why she did not answer me but instead showed me a random music box!"

"The girl told me to play it if I wanted the 'truth.' I didn't know what that meant, but I didn't want to leave there empty-handed. As I played it, I heard someone singing. That was when I noticed a familiar tone within the song. Then it hit me. If the singer had the same voice as the ghost girl, was I in the presence of Rose? Once I realized that, I wanted to ask her many questions but the song ended and she had already disappeared."

After he said that, everyone else went silent and took a moment to recollect their thoughts.

"Okay, I think we're fine now. So, why did the queen bring you that scroll?" asked Thomas as he kept staring at the artifact.

"Oh! You see, I studied both the map and the message. I then realized it was an assignment to find the Night Demon and bring him to her," explained the Professor.

After planning what they will do once they find the demon, everyone finished their dinner and got ready for bed. Lindy was trying to sleep but she kept thinking about today's events. After thinking about it some more, something in her mind finally convinced her to go.

"What are you waiting for? Let's go demon hunting!"

Author's Note:

Hello Everyone! My name is Destinee Munoz, and I'm an aspiring author. This is my first book that I have written and it is the first book in a new series. I'll also be writing horror books so keep an eye out for that!

The inspiration behind my novels are: my family, my favorite voice actors, Kyzer Aqueron and voices, DarkBox, ect!

I first want to thank my family for encouraging me to write and for giving me ideas for my future new books. I also want to thank Kyzer Aqueron and my other favorite Youtubers for inspiring and motivating me every single day.

Made in the USA
Monee, IL
12 February 2021

60383304R00035